Deception in Bloom

Nazreen zainab

Published by Nazreen zainab, 2024.

This is a work of fiction. Similarities to real people, places, or events are entirely coincidental.

DECEPTION IN BLOOM

First edition. September 3, 2024.

Copyright © 2024 Nazreen zainab.

ISBN: 979-8227520739

Written by Nazreen zainab.

Chapter 1

The Blind Date Debacle

Scene 1: The Setup

Cat Sinclair sat at the small, tastefully decorated table, drumming her fingers against the polished surface as she glanced at the door for the tenth time in the last minute. She was in one of the trendiest restaurants in town, "Le Petit Jardin," known for its quaint atmosphere and over-the-top romantic ambiance. Soft jazz music floated through the air, and couples filled every table, bathed in the warm glow of candlelight. It was the kind of place that practically screamed "first date," which was ironic since Cat had sworn off dating just a few weeks earlier.

But here she was, on a blind date set up by her well-meaning but meddlesome best friend, Maggie.

Maggie was always on the lookout for potential love interests for Cat, convinced that her best friend's single status was some kind of emergency that needed immediate rectification. After months of pestering, Cat had finally caved in, more to get Maggie off her back than anything else.

As the minutes ticked by, Cat's initial irritation began to give way to full-blown annoyance. She checked her phone again, even though there were no new messages. Her date was officially fifteen minutes late.

"Typical," she muttered to herself, taking a sip of her wine. It was an excellent vintage, but tonight it tasted like disappointment.

Cat wasn't desperate for a relationship—far from it. She had a fulfilling career as an event planner, a close-knit group of friends, and a cozy apartment that she adored. But there was something undeniably lonely about being the only single person at every gathering. So, she'd allowed Maggie to talk her into this, even though her instincts had screamed at her to decline.

SCENE 2: THE DATE FROM Hell

When the restaurant door finally opened, Cat looked up, her heart doing a little flip in her chest. But her hopeful anticipation quickly fizzled when she saw a man who looked nothing like the description Maggie had given her. Instead of the charming, confident gentleman she'd been promised, this man looked... well, disheveled.

He was tall but lanky, with a mop of unruly hair that seemed to have a life of its own. His clothes were wrinkled, and his tie was askew as if he'd just thrown it on in the cab ride over. Worse, he had a deer-in-the-headlights expression that immediately set off alarm bells in Cat's head.

"Are you Cat?" he asked nervously, approaching her table.

She forced a smile and nodded. "That's me."

"Sorry, I'm late. Traffic was a nightmare." He slid into the seat across from her, knocking over the water glass as he did so. "Oh, crap!"

Cat watched as he scrambled to right the glass, water spreading across the tablecloth like a slow-moving disaster. The waiter hurried over, looking both annoyed and sympathetic as he mopped up the spill and brought a new glass.

"No worries," Cat said, trying to keep her tone light. "It happens."

"I'm Greg," he said, finally settling in. "Greg Townsend. Maggie told me a lot about you."

Cat nodded politely, though her patience was already wearing thin. "She did? Well, I hope she wasn't too generous with the details."

Greg chuckled awkwardly, and Cat felt a pang of guilt for being so judgmental. Maybe she was being too harsh—after all, first dates were nerve-wracking, and not everyone handled them well.

But as the evening progressed, it became clear that Greg's nerves were just the tip of the iceberg. He rambled on about his job in IT, which might have been interesting if he hadn't been so dry and technical about it. Every attempt Cat made to steer the conversation toward lighter, more engaging topics was met with long-winded explanations about software algorithms or network security protocols.

Cat tried to keep her mind from wandering, but it was no use. Her thoughts drifted to work, to her friends, and finally to the ridiculousness of the situation. By the time the main course arrived, she was barely able to conceal her boredom.

Greg, oblivious to her disinterest, continued to drone on. He didn't ask her a single question about herself, and any time she tried to contribute to the conversation, he interrupted her to continue his monologue.

SCENE 3: THE ESCAPE Plan

Cat's breaking point came during dessert. As Greg launched into a detailed explanation of the latest cybersecurity breach in his company, Cat couldn't take it anymore. She needed to get out—now.

Feigning an apologetic smile, she interrupted him. "Greg, I'm so sorry, but I just remembered I have an early morning meeting tomorrow. I really need to cut this short."

Greg blinked, surprised, and for a moment, Cat felt a twinge of guilt. But it was quickly overshadowed by her overwhelming need to escape.

"Oh, sure," Greg stammered, clearly taken aback. "I didn't realize it was so late."

Cat quickly signalled for the check, determined to split it and make a swift exit. As she fumbled in her purse for her wallet, Greg's hand shot out to stop her.

"No, let me," he insisted, his earlier nervousness returning full force. "I'll cover it."

Cat hesitated, then nodded gratefully. "Thank you."

They waited in awkward silence for the waiter to return, and when he did, Greg paid the bill with shaking hands. Cat felt a pang of sympathy for him—it wasn't his fault that the date had been a disaster. He'd just been the wrong guy at the wrong time.

As they stepped out into the cool night air, Cat forced a smile. "Thanks for dinner, Greg. It was... interesting."

"Yeah, it was," Greg agreed, clearly unsure how to interpret her words. "Maybe we could do it again sometime?"

Cat froze. The thought of another evening like this one was enough to make her want to crawl into bed and never leave. But she didn't want to hurt his feelings.

"We'll see," she said diplomatically, giving him a quick hug before turning and walking away.

SCENE 4: THE DIVE BAR

Cat hurried down the street, eager to put as much distance between herself and the restaurant as possible. She knew she should just go home and chalk the evening up to experience, but she wasn't ready to face the quiet of her apartment just yet. She needed a drink—something strong to wash away the bad taste of the night.

As if answering her unspoken wish, she spotted a small, dimly lit bar on the corner. The neon sign above the door simply read "Murphy's." It was the kind of place that looked like it had seen better days, but right now, it was exactly what Cat needed.

She pushed open the door and stepped inside, immediately enveloped by the low hum of conversation and the smell of stale beer. The place was almost empty, save for a few regulars nursing their drinks at the bar. It was a far cry from the upscale restaurant she'd just left, but it felt oddly comforting.

Cat slid onto a barstool and ordered a whiskey, savouring the burn as she took her first sip. She could feel the tension in her shoulders start to melt away, and for the first time all evening, she allowed herself to relax.

She was halfway through her drink when the bar door opened again, and in walked a man who immediately caught her attention.

Tall, with broad shoulders and an easy confidence, he had the kind of presence that was impossible to ignore. He wore a leather jacket over a simple t-shirt and jeans, but something about the way he carried himself made him stand out. His dark hair was tousled just enough to look effortlessly cool, and his sharp blue eyes scanned the room before settling on her.

To her surprise, he walked straight over and took the seat next to her.

"Rough night?" he asked, his voice deep and smooth.

Cat looked at him, half in disbelief. Was this guy for real? He looked like he'd just stepped out of a magazine spread.

"You could say that," she replied cautiously, taking another sip of her whiskey.

He nodded, signalling the bartender for a drink. "Let me guess—a blind date gone wrong?"

Cat stared at him, startled. "How did you know?"

He shrugged, a hint of a smile playing at the corners of his mouth. "Lucky guess. You've got that look—like you're ready to throw in the towel on the whole dating thing."

She couldn't help but laugh. "You have no idea."

"Try me," he said, turning to face her fully. "I'm Ryan, by the way."

"Cat," she replied, feeling a warmth that had nothing to do with the whiskey. "And trust me, Ryan, you don't want to hear about my night."

Ryan raised an eyebrow, clearly intrigued. "I think I might."

For reasons she couldn't quite explain, Cat found herself telling him everything—the blind date disaster, Greg's endless tech talk, and her desperate need to escape. Ryan listened with a combination of amusement and sympathy, and by the time she finished, she felt like a weight had been lifted off her shoulders.

"You know what you need?" Ryan said when she was done. "You need to forget about tonight and have some fun. What do you say? One night, no strings attached—just a couple of drinks and some good company."

Cat hesitated, but there was something about Ryan that made her want to throw caution to the wind. He was charming, yes, but there was also a mischievous spark in his eyes that made her think he might be just what she needed

Chapter 2

The Chemistry and the Red Flags

Scene 1: **The Spark**

It had been two weeks since that chance meeting with Ryan at Murphy's, and in that short time, Cat Sinclair felt as though her life had shifted in ways she hadn't anticipated. What had started as a night of impulsive drinks and flirty banter had quickly evolved into something more—a whirlwind romance that made her feel like she was living in a romantic comedy. Ryan Winters was everything Greg Townsend wasn't: confident, charming, and effortlessly cool.

He had a way of making her feel like she was the only woman in the room, and every time they were together, sparks seemed to fly between them. From the stolen glances to the playful teasing, their chemistry was undeniable. Cat found herself thinking about him constantly, replaying their conversations in her mind and reliving the moments when he'd made her laugh or smile.

But as much as she enjoyed the rush of excitement that came with being around Ryan, there was a nagging voice in the back of her mind that she couldn't quite silence. Something about him didn't add up.

That evening, as she stood in front of the mirror in her small but stylish apartment, adjusting her dress and applying the final touches to her makeup, Cat couldn't help but feel a flutter of nerves. She was meeting Ryan for dinner at a trendy new restaurant that had just opened downtown. It was their fifth date in two weeks, and despite her growing feelings for him, she couldn't shake the sense that there were things about Ryan that didn't quite add up.

For one, she still didn't know much about his work. He'd mentioned being involved in the tech industry, but every time she tried to ask him about his business, he brushed off the question with a vague answer and changed the subject. He also had a habit of disappearing for long stretches during the day, claiming to be "caught up in work," but offering no details.

Still, Cat couldn't deny how much fun she had with him. He made her feel alive in a way she hadn't felt in years—maybe ever. And tonight, as she smoothed down her dress and took one last look in the mirror, she decided to push her doubts aside. Maybe she was overthinking things. Maybe she just needed to let herself enjoy the moment.

When she arrived at the restaurant, Ryan was already waiting for her at the bar, looking as effortlessly handsome as ever. He flashed her that signature smile as she approached, and all her worries seemed to melt away.

"You look stunning," he said, pulling her into a warm embrace. His lips brushed against her cheek, and she felt a rush of warmth spread through her body.

"You're not so bad yourself," Cat replied with a playful grin, feeling her heart race as he took her hand and led her to their table.

SCENE 2: A NIGHT OF Laughter and Unanswered Questions

Dinner with Ryan was, as always, a mixture of flirtation, laughter, and easy conversation. He had a way of making even the most mundane topics feel interesting, and Cat found herself hanging on his every word. The way he spoke, with such confidence and charm, made it easy to forget her earlier doubts.

"So, how was your day?" Ryan asked as the waiter poured them both glasses of wine.

"Busy," Cat replied, sipping her wine and feeling the familiar warmth spread through her chest. "I'm working on a big event for a client—a corporate gala for one of the tech companies in town. It's been a bit of a headache, but nothing I can't handle."

Ryan raised an eyebrow, a glimmer of amusement in his eyes. "A tech company, huh? Maybe I should give you some insider tips."

Cat laughed. "Oh, please do. I'm sure the CEO would love to hear that I have an anonymous source feeding me industry secrets."

Ryan chuckled, but once again, when the conversation shifted toward his own work, he seemed to steer it in a different direction. Cat found herself watching him more closely, noting the way he deflected her questions with charm and wit. It was almost as if he was playing a game—a game she hadn't quite figured out yet.

As the evening wore on, Cat couldn't help but feel a sense of déjà vu. It was the same pattern every time: they would laugh, flirt, and enjoy each other's company, but when it came to anything deeper—anything personal—Ryan was an enigma. He never talked about his family, his past, or his friends. He was a mystery wrapped in a charming smile and a well-tailored suit.

And yet, despite the red flags, Cat found herself drawn to him more and more with each passing day. There was something intoxicating about the way he looked at her, the way he made her feel like she was the most important person in the world. It was the kind of chemistry that was hard to ignore, even when her instincts told her to be cautious.

By the time they finished dinner and stepped out into the cool night air, Cat's mind was buzzing with a mixture of excitement and uncertainty. Ryan slipped his arm around her waist as they walked down the street, and for a moment, she let herself forget about her doubts. She leaned into him, feeling the warmth of his body against hers.

"You want to come back to my place for a drink?" Ryan asked, his voice low and suggestive.

Cat hesitated for a moment, her heart racing. She knew where this was headed, and as much as she wanted to take things to the next level with Ryan, she also couldn't shake the feeling that there were things about him she still didn't know.

But tonight, she didn't want to think about that. Tonight, she just wanted to enjoy the moment.

"Yeah," she said with a smile. "I'd like that."

SCENE 3: THE MORNING After

The next morning, Cat woke up in Ryan's bed, sunlight streaming through the curtains. She stretched, feeling the pleasant ache in her muscles from the night before. Ryan was still asleep beside her, his arm draped over her waist. For a moment, Cat just lay there, listening to the sound of his steady breathing and feeling the warmth of his body against hers.

It had been a perfect night. After they'd gotten back to his place, they'd shared a bottle of wine, talked, and laughed some more before things had taken a more intimate turn. Cat couldn't remember the last time she'd felt so connected to someone—so completely at ease in their presence.

But as she lay there, the nagging doubts from the night before began to creep back in. She still didn't know much about Ryan, and the more time they spent together, the more she realized how little he revealed about himself. It was almost as if he was deliberately keeping her at arm's length, only letting her see the parts of him that he wanted her to see.

She shifted in bed, careful not to wake him, and reached for her phone on the nightstand. There were a few texts from Maggie, her best friend, asking how the date had gone. Cat smiled to herself as she typed out a quick reply, telling Maggie that it had been amazing.

As she set her phone back down, she couldn't help but glance at Ryan's phone, which was lying face down on the nightstand next to hers. She'd never been one to snoop, but a part of her was curious. What was he hiding? Why did he always seem so secretive?

Before she could stop herself, Cat reached for Ryan's phone, her heart racing as she flipped it over. But just as she was about to unlock it, Ryan stirred beside her, his arm tightening around her waist.

"Good morning," he murmured, his voice thick with sleep.

Cat quickly set the phone back down, feeling a rush of guilt. "Good morning," she replied, turning to face him.

Ryan smiled at her, his eyes still half-closed. "Last night was incredible," he said, leaning in to kiss her.

Cat smiled, her doubts temporarily forgotten as she kissed him back. "It really was."

For the rest of the morning, they lounged in bed, talking and laughing as if they didn't have a care in the world. Ryan made them coffee and breakfast, and for a little while, Cat allowed herself to believe that everything was perfect.

But as the day went on and she headed back to her apartment, the doubts began to creep back in. She couldn't ignore the red flags any longer—there were too many unanswered questions, too many things about Ryan that didn't add up.

And yet, despite all of that, Cat couldn't help but feel drawn to him. There was something about him that made her want to believe in him, to trust that he was the man he appeared to be. But deep down, she knew that trust had to be earned—and Ryan hadn't quite earned it yet.

SCENE 4: THE FIRST Real Fight

Later that week, Cat and Ryan made plans to meet for drinks at a trendy rooftop bar downtown. The evening started out as usual—light hearted and fun—but as the night wore on, the tension that had been building between them finally came to a head.

It started with a seemingly innocent question. Cat had asked Ryan about his day, and once again, he gave her a vague answer, brushing off the details with a charming smile.

But this time, Cat didn't let it slide.

"Ryan, why don't you ever talk about your work?" she asked, her tone more serious than she intended.

Ryan looked at her, his smile faltering for a moment. "I've told you, Cat. It's just... complicated."

"Complicated how?" Cat pressed. "I mean, you've told me you're in tech, but you never give me any specifics

Chapter 3

Falling Fast

Scene 1: A Weekend Away

A few weeks after their first real fight, Ryan suggested they get out of the city for a weekend, just the two of them. Cat hesitated at first, still wary after their argument, but she eventually agreed. The idea of spending a few days in a secluded cabin in the woods, far away from the stress of work and the constant red flags she'd been trying to ignore, was tempting. It could be a fresh start, she told herself—a chance to truly get to know Ryan without all the distractions of their busy lives.

The drive up to the cabin was idyllic, the scenery turning from the bustling cityscape to peaceful, tree-lined roads. Ryan had picked out a charming little cabin by the lake, and as they pulled up, Cat couldn't help but be impressed. The cabin looked straight out of a postcard, with its rustic wooden exterior and large windows that offered stunning views of the surrounding forest.

"This place is beautiful," Cat said as they stepped out of the car. She stretched her arms above her head, breathing in the crisp, fresh air.

"I thought you'd like it," Ryan replied, smiling as he grabbed their bags from the trunk. "No cell service, no interruptions. Just us."

Cat smiled back, feeling a sense of calm wash over her. Maybe this was exactly what they needed—a break from the outside world, a chance to focus on each other. She wanted to believe that this weekend could help her put her doubts to rest once and for all.

Inside the cabin, everything was just as charming as the outside. There was a cozy fireplace in the living room, a small but well-equipped kitchen, and a bedroom with large windows that looked out over the lake. Ryan immediately got to work building a fire, while Cat unpacked their bags and poured them both a glass of wine.

Once the fire was crackling, they settled onto the couch, their legs entwined as they sipped their wine and talked about nothing in particular. The tension from their previous argument seemed to melt away, and for the first time in weeks, Cat felt like she could truly relax.

Ryan had that effect on her—when they were together like this, with no distractions, it was easy to forget about the red flags. He was attentive, affectionate, and always made her feel like she was the center of his world. It was one of the reasons she had fallen for him so quickly. But there was still that nagging voice in the back of her mind, reminding her that there were things about him she didn't know—things he was deliberately keeping from her.

But tonight, Cat pushed those thoughts aside. She wanted to enjoy this weekend, to fall deeper into the feelings she had for him without letting her doubts ruin it.

"To us," Ryan said, raising his glass.

"To us," Cat echoed, clinking her glass against his.

As the fire crackled and the wine flowed, they leaned into each other, their lips meeting in a slow, lingering kiss. It wasn't long before the rest of the world faded away, and it was just the two of them, wrapped in each other's arms.

Scene 2: The Illusion of Perfection

The weekend passed in a blissful haze of long walks by the lake, late-night conversations by the fire, and passionate moments that left Cat breathless. Every time she looked at Ryan, she felt herself falling deeper into him, drawn in by his charm, his confidence, and the way he made her feel like she was the only person that mattered.

They cooked meals together in the small kitchen, laughed over old stories, and shared bits and pieces of their lives that they hadn't discussed before. Ryan opened up more than he ever had, telling Cat about his childhood, his dreams, and even a few anecdotes from his work in tech—though they were still frustratingly vague.

Despite the lingering doubts in the back of her mind, Cat found herself feeling more connected to Ryan than ever. It was easy to get lost in the illusion of perfection that this weekend had created. Out here, away from the city and the daily grind, everything felt simpler, easier. It was as if the real world didn't exist, and they were living in their own little bubble of happiness.

But even as she allowed herself to get swept up in the romance of it all, Cat couldn't completely ignore the subtle undercurrent of tension that occasionally surfaced. There were moments when Ryan seemed distant, lost in his own thoughts, and when she asked him about it, he would brush it off with a charming smile or a quick kiss.

At one point, during a particularly beautiful sunset, Cat found herself watching Ryan as he stared out over the lake, his expression unreadable.

"What are you thinking about?" she asked, sliding her arm around his waist.

Ryan glanced down at her and smiled, but there was something guarded in his eyes. "Just... life," he said vaguely. "You know, the usual stuff."

Cat frowned, sensing that he was holding something back, but she didn't press him. Instead, she leaned her head against his shoulder and watched the sun dip below the horizon, painting the sky in shades of pink and orange.

She wanted to believe that this was real—that the connection they had was strong enough to overcome the doubts she had about him. But deep down, she knew that the illusion of perfection couldn't last forever.

SCENE 3: CRACKS IN the Facade

The weekend ended too soon, and as they drove back to the city, Cat found herself feeling both exhilarated and anxious. The time they had spent together had been magical, but as they returned to their normal lives, the nagging doubts began to resurface.

A few days after they got back, Cat received a text from Maggie, asking how the weekend had gone. Cat hesitated before replying, unsure of how to describe the experience. On the surface, everything had been perfect, but there was still that lingering sense that something wasn't quite right.

It was amazing, she finally typed back. *But I still feel like there are things he's not telling me.*

Maggie responded almost immediately. *That's because there probably are. Trust your gut, Cat. If something feels off, it probably is.*

Cat sighed as she stared at her phone. She knew Maggie was right—her best friend had always had a knack for seeing things clearly, even when Cat couldn't. But at the same time, Cat didn't want to let her doubts ruin what could be an incredible relationship.

That evening, Cat and Ryan had plans to meet for dinner, but at the last minute, Ryan called to cancel.

"Work emergency," he said over the phone, his voice rushed. "I'm really sorry, but I have to deal with this. Rain check?"

Cat tried to hide her disappointment. "Of course. Let me know if you need anything."

"Thanks, Cat. You're the best."

After they hung up, Cat sat on her couch, staring at her phone. She trusted him—she wanted to trust him—but this wasn't the first time he had canceled plans at the last minute for vague "work emergencies." It was becoming a pattern, and Cat couldn't help but wonder if there was more to it than he was letting on.

The next day, Cat decided to do something she had never done before in any relationship: she Googled him.

At first, she didn't find much—just a few professional profiles that seemed legitimate enough. But as she dug deeper, she started to uncover small inconsistencies in his story. There were mentions of past companies he'd supposedly worked for that didn't seem to exist, and some of his online profiles listed job titles that didn't match what he'd told her.

The more she searched, the more uneasy she felt. It wasn't enough to accuse him of anything, but it was enough to make her question everything.

Scene 4: Confrontation

A few days later, Cat decided it was time to confront Ryan. She couldn't go on pretending everything was fine when she knew deep down that something wasn't right. If they were going to have a real future together, she needed answers—and she needed them now.

They met for dinner at a cozy little Italian restaurant that Ryan had suggested. As they sat across from each other, the candlelight flickering between them, Cat could feel the tension in the air. She tried to make small talk, but her mind kept drifting back to the questions she had been holding onto for weeks.

Finally, she couldn't take it anymore.

"Ryan," she said, setting her fork down and looking him in the eye. "I need to ask you something, and I want you to be honest with me."

Ryan raised an eyebrow, clearly sensing the seriousness of her tone. "Of course. What's on your mind?"

Cat took a deep breath, steeling herself for what she was about to say. "I've been feeling like there are things you're not telling me—about your work, your life... everything. I don't want to sound paranoid, but I need to know that I can trust you."

Ryan's expression softened, and for a moment, Cat thought he might finally open up. But instead, he reached across the table and took her hand, his thumb brushing gently against her skin.

"Cat, I get it," he said quietly. "I know I haven't been as open as I should be, and I'm sorry for that. But I promise you, there's nothing shady going on. My work can be... complicated, and sometimes I can't share all the details. But that doesn't mean I don't care about you." Cat stared at him, trying to read the sincerity in his eyes. She wanted to believe him she really did. But there was still a part of her that couldn't shake the reality

Chapter 4

Doubts and Deceptions

Scene 1: Suspicion Creeping In

Two months into her relationship with Ryan, Cat could no longer ignore the uneasy feeling that had settled in the pit of her stomach. No matter how much she tried to convince herself that Ryan's charm and warmth outweighed the uncertainties, her mind kept circling back to the unanswered questions and the red flags that continued to pop up.

She had hoped their weekend away would bring them closer together, and while it had been a brief escape into romance, it hadn't erased the gnawing sense that something wasn't quite right. The more time she spent with Ryan, the more she realized that she didn't really know him at all.

Ryan continued to be vague about his work, and though Cat had tried to let it go, the inconsistencies in his stories were becoming too glaring to ignore. He claimed to be involved in tech, yet he never spoke in specifics. There were days when he would disappear for hours, sometimes even a full day, only to return with little explanation. His excuses ranged from "business meetings" to "last-minute deals," but Cat had begun to wonder if those were simply covers for something else—something he didn't want her to know.

One evening, as they sat in Ryan's apartment after dinner, Cat watched him as he scrolled through his phone. He seemed distracted, his brow furrowed in concentration, and when she asked him about it, he quickly locked his screen and set his phone face down on the coffee table.

"Just work stuff," he said, flashing her that disarming smile that always made her heart flutter. "Nothing exciting."

But Cat wasn't convinced. The secrecy around his phone had become another point of tension between them. Ryan never left it unattended, and whenever she was around, he made sure it was either face down or in his pocket. Cat had even noticed that he'd disabled the preview notifications on his messages, making it impossible to see who was texting him without unlocking the device.

She didn't want to be that girlfriend—the one who snooped and pried into her partner's personal life—but at the same time, she couldn't shake the feeling that Ryan was hiding something. And the more he kept things from her, the more she began to doubt the entire foundation of their relationship.

One night, after Ryan had fallen asleep beside her, Cat lay awake in bed, staring at the ceiling and replaying the events of the past few weeks in her mind. She thought about the way he always seemed to dodge her questions, the way he deflected any conversation that veered into personal territory, and the way he always had an excuse for his absences.

Cat had never been the type to doubt her instincts, but when it came to Ryan, she found herself second-guessing everything. Was she being paranoid, or was there really something sinister lurking beneath the surface? She needed to know the truth, even if it meant confronting the possibility that Ryan wasn't the man she thought he was.

SCENE 2: THE UNRAVELLING Begins

The following week, Cat decided to take matters into her own hands. She couldn't continue living in this limbo of doubt and suspicion, constantly wondering if Ryan was being honest with her. If he wasn't going to give her the answers she needed, she would have to find them herself.

She started small—paying closer attention to the details of his stories, looking for any discrepancies that might point to a lie. And it didn't take long for her to notice the cracks.

One evening, after Ryan had cancelled their plans for the second time that week, Cat decided to dig a little deeper into his past. She sat down at her computer and pulled up the search engine, typing in his name and scrolling through the results. Most of what she found was fairly innocuous—social media profiles, LinkedIn pages, and the occasional mention in tech-related articles. But the more she searched, the more she realized that Ryan's online presence was strangely limited for someone who claimed to be involved in a high-level tech career.

There were no interviews, no articles featuring him as a thought leader in the industry, no company website listing him as a founder or executive. It was almost as if Ryan Winters didn't exist beyond the few carefully curated profiles he had online.

Cat's heart raced as she clicked through page after page of search results, her mind racing with possibilities. What if Ryan wasn't who he said he was? What if he was hiding something—something big?

But just as she was about to give up and close her laptop, she stumbled across something that made her blood run cold.

It was a forum post, buried deep in the recesses of the internet, from a woman named Jessica who described a relationship eerily similar to Cat's. She wrote about a man she had met through mutual friends—charming, mysterious, and vague about his work in tech. He had swept her off her feet, only to vanish after a few months, leaving her with more questions than answers.

The details were too similar to ignore. The way he had deflected questions about his job, the way he had disappeared without explanation, the way he had kept his phone locked and guarded at all times—it was all there, in black and white.

Cat's hands trembled as she scrolled through the post, her heart pounding in her chest. Could this be Ryan? Could he have done this before, to other women?

She needed to find out more. She needed to know if the man she had fallen for was the same man who had left this woman heartbroken and confused.

SCENE 3: CONFRONTING the Truth

The next day, Cat couldn't focus at work. Her mind was consumed with thoughts of Ryan and the forum post she had found. She kept replaying their conversations in her head, analysing every word, every glance, every moment when he had seemed evasive or distant.

By the time she got home that evening, she was determined to confront him. She couldn't keep living in this state of doubt—she needed answers, and she needed them now.

Ryan was coming over for dinner, and as Cat waited for him to arrive, she paced nervously around her apartment, rehearsing what she would say. She didn't want to jump to conclusions or accuse him of something he hadn't done, but at the same time, she couldn't ignore the mounting evidence that suggested he was hiding something from her.

When Ryan finally arrived, Cat greeted him with a forced smile, her heart pounding in her chest. They sat down to eat, and for a while, everything seemed normal—too normal. Ryan was his usual charming self, making small talk and cracking jokes, completely unaware of the storm brewing inside Cat's mind.

But Cat couldn't keep up the charade for long. As soon as they finished dinner, she set her fork down and took a deep breath.

"Ryan, we need to talk."

Ryan looked up at her, his expression softening as he sensed the seriousness in her tone. "What's going on?"

Cat hesitated for a moment, unsure of how to begin. But then she remembered the forum post, the woman who had been in her exact situation, and the words came tumbling out.

"I've been having doubts," she said, her voice shaking slightly. "I feel like there are things you're not telling me—about your work, your past... everything. And I found something online—a post from a woman who described a relationship that sounds almost exactly like ours. She said the man she was with disappeared without a trace after a few months, and I can't help but wonder... is that you?"

Ryan's expression darkened, and for a moment, Cat saw a flicker of something she hadn't seen before—something cold and calculating.

"Cat," he said slowly, his voice dangerously calm. "I can't believe you'd even think that."

"I'm sorry," Cat said, her heart racing. "But I had to ask. You've been so secretive about everything, and I've been trying to ignore it, but I can't anymore. I need to know the truth."

Ryan's jaw clenched, and he stood up from the table, pacing across the room as he ran a hand through his hair.

"You're paranoid," he said, his voice tight with frustration. "I've told you everything I can about my work. It's not my fault if you can't handle the fact that I have to keep some things private."

Cat felt a surge of anger rise within her. "This isn't about your work, Ryan. This is about trust. How can I trust you when you won't even let me in?"

Ryan stopped pacing and turned to face her, his eyes flashing with something dark and unreadable. "Maybe you're the one who doesn't deserve my trust," he said coldly.

Cat recoiled as if she had been slapped. For a moment, neither of them spoke, the air between them thick with tension.

Finally, Ryan sighed and rubbed his temples, as if trying to regain his composure. "Look," he said more softly. "I care about you, Cat. I do. But you have to understand that there are things I can't share with you—things that are out of my control."

Cat stared at him, her mind racing. Was he telling the truth, or was this just another carefully constructed lie?

"Then prove it," she said quietly. "Prove to me that you're not hiding anything."

Ryan hesitated for a moment, then slowly nodded. "Okay," he said. "I'll show you. But you have to promise me that you'll trust me after this."

Cat nodded, though she wasn't sure if she could make that promise.

Ryan reached into his pocket and pulled out his phone, unlocking it before handing it to her. "Look,"

Chapter 5

The Mask Slips

SCENE 1: UNVEILING Secrets

Cat stared down at Ryan's phone, her hands trembling slightly as she took it from him. This was the moment she had been waiting for—the moment where she would finally get answers, where all of her doubts would either be dispelled or confirmed.

"Go ahead," Ryan said, watching her intently. "Check whatever you need to check. You'll see I'm not hiding anything."

Cat's stomach twisted with anxiety. She didn't want to be this person—someone who snooped through her boyfriend's phone, invading his privacy. But the stakes felt too high. Her future with Ryan, her sense of trust, even her own peace of mind—all of it depended on what she found here.

She started by scrolling through his messages. At first, everything seemed normal—casual conversations with co-workers, texts from friends, and even a few sweet exchanges between the two of them. Nothing seemed out of place. But then, as she scrolled further, she noticed a contact she didn't recognize: "M. Johnson."

Her heart raced as she opened the thread, half expecting to find something incriminating. But instead, the messages were brief and business-like. They discussed meetings, locations, and timelines, but without context, they were hard to decipher. Nothing about the conversation indicated anything romantic or personal, but the tone was cryptic enough to make her suspicious.

"Who's M. Johnson?" Cat asked, looking up at Ryan.

Ryan crossed his arms over his chest, his expression unreadable. "He's a business associate. We've been working on a project together for a while now."

Cat narrowed her eyes. "What kind of project?"

Ryan hesitated for a split second before answering. "It's confidential. I can't get into the details."

There it was again—the same vague deflection he always gave her when she pressed too hard. Cat clenched her jaw in frustration. She wanted to believe him, but the more he withheld from her, the more she felt like he was constructing a wall between them.

"You see?" Ryan said, his voice softening. "There's nothing to worry about. I'm not hiding anything."

Cat frowned, handing the phone back to him. The messages hadn't given her the clarity she was looking for, but something still felt off. It wasn't what she had found that concerned her—it was what she hadn't found. The way Ryan kept so much of his life cloaked in mystery, the way he always seemed to give just enough information to pacify her without ever really revealing anything.

"I don't know, Ryan," Cat said, her voice tinged with uncertainty. "I just feel like you're keeping me at arm's length. And that's not how relationships are supposed to work."

Ryan stepped closer to her, his hand reaching out to cup her face. His touch was warm, but his eyes were cold. "I told you, Cat, there are things I can't share. You have to trust me on that. But that doesn't mean I don't care about you."

Cat swallowed hard, her throat tight with emotion. She wanted so desperately to believe him, to trust that everything he was saying was true. But deep down, she knew that something wasn't right. The cracks in his story were growing wider, and she could feel the foundation of their relationship starting to crumble beneath her feet.

Scene 2: The Lie Exposed

A week passed, and despite Ryan's reassurances, Cat couldn't shake the feeling that he was lying to her. She tried to push the doubts to the back of her mind, but they gnawed at her, creeping into her thoughts when she least expected them. Every time Ryan cancelled plans or gave her another vague excuse about work, her suspicions grew stronger.

One evening, after Ryan had once again claimed to be tied up in a "work meeting," Cat decided she couldn't take it anymore. She had to know the truth, even if it meant crossing a line she wasn't comfortable with. So she did something she had sworn she would never do—she followed him.

It wasn't hard to find him. Ryan had told her he would be at a restaurant downtown for a business dinner, and Cat knew the place well. She waited outside in her car, watching the entrance with a mixture of guilt and determination. This wasn't who she wanted to be, but she couldn't continue living in this state of uncertainty.

An hour passed, and Cat was beginning to think she had made a mistake. Maybe Ryan really was in a meeting—maybe she was being paranoid. But just as she was about to leave, she saw him.

Ryan emerged from the restaurant, not with a group of co-workers as she had expected, but with a woman. She was tall and elegant, her hair swept back in a chic bun, and she was laughing at something Ryan had said. Cat's heart plummeted as she watched them. Ryan had his arm around the woman's waist, and there was an intimacy between them that Cat had never seen before.

They walked down the street together, and Cat followed at a safe distance, her mind racing. Who was this woman? What was Ryan doing with her? And why had he lied to Cat about where he was?

As they walked further, Cat's suspicions were confirmed. Ryan wasn't just having dinner with this woman—he was clearly involved with her.

The way he touched her, the way he leaned in close to whisper in her ear—it was undeniable. Cat's stomach churned with a mixture of anger and heartbreak. She had been right all along. Ryan had been lying to her, hiding a whole other life that she knew nothing about.

She followed them for several blocks, her emotions swinging wildly between disbelief and fury. How could he do this to her? How could he stand there, look her in the eyes, and tell her that he cared about her while sneaking around with another woman?

Finally, they stopped outside an apartment building. Ryan pulled the woman in for a kiss, and Cat felt a wave of nausea wash over her. She couldn't watch anymore. She turned and walked away, her mind reeling with the realization that the man she had fallen for was nothing but a liar.

SCENE 3: CONFRONTATION and Denial

The next day, Cat couldn't hold it in any longer. She had spent the entire night replaying the scene in her head, trying to make sense of everything. But no matter how hard she tried, she couldn't come up with a logical explanation for Ryan's behavior. There was only one conclusion—he had been cheating on her.

She decided to confront him.

They met at a café, and Ryan greeted her with a smile, as if nothing was wrong. But Cat could barely look at him without feeling a surge of anger and betrayal.

"We need to talk," she said, her voice tight with emotion.

Ryan frowned, sensing the tension in her tone. "What's wrong?"

Cat took a deep breath, trying to steady her nerves. "I know about the woman, Ryan. I saw you with her last night."

Ryan's eyes widened in shock, and for a moment, he looked genuinely stunned. "What? Cat, no—"

"Don't lie to me!" Cat snapped, her voice rising. "I followed you. I saw you with her. You were supposed to be at a work dinner, but instead, you were out with her. I watched you kiss her, Ryan. Don't even try to deny it."

Ryan stared at her, his face pale. For a moment, he said nothing, and Cat could see the wheels turning in his mind as he tried to figure out how to respond.

Finally, he sighed, running a hand through his hair. "Cat... I can explain."

"Explain?" Cat's voice was incredulous. "What is there to explain? You've been lying to me for weeks, Ryan. You've been sneaking around with another woman while telling me that you care about me. How could you do this?"

Ryan's expression shifted, and for a brief moment, the mask he had worn so carefully began to slip. There was something cold in his eyes, something calculating.

"I didn't want to hurt you," he said, his voice devoid of emotion. "I never meant for things to get this complicated."

"Complicated?" Cat felt like she was going to explode. "You were cheating on me, Ryan! This isn't complicated—it's betrayal!"

Ryan's jaw tightened, and for the first time since she had known him, Cat saw a side of him that frightened her. There was no remorse in his eyes, no regret for what he had done. Instead, there was a cold detachment, as if he didn't care about the pain he had caused her.

"I told you before," Ryan said, his voice low and dangerous. "There are things I can't share with you. Things that are bigger than you or me."

Cat stared at him, her heart breaking all over again. "What are you talking about?"

Ryan shook his head. "You wouldn't understand."

"Then help me understand," Cat pleaded. "Tell me the truth, Ryan. Who is she? What's going on?"

Ryan's expression hardened. "It's better if you don't know."

Cat felt tears sting her eyes as she realized that this was it. There would be no explanation, no closure. Ryan had lied to her, betrayed her, and now he was refusing to even take responsibility for it.

"I can't do this anymore," she said, her voice shaking. "I'm done, Ryan. We're done."

For a moment, Ryan looked like he might say something, but then he simply nodded, his expression unreadable. "If that's what you want."

Cat stood up and left the cafe

Chapter 6

Love and Lies

Scene 1: The Aftermath

After Cat walked out of the café, she felt the world around her spin in slow motion. She had broken up with Ryan—the man she had once thought might be "the one." The man who had swept her off her feet, only to shatter her trust with lies and betrayal. She replayed his cold, detached expression in her mind, and it sent a chill down her spine. This wasn't the man she had fallen for, and yet, it had always been him, hiding behind a mask of charm and affection.

Cat spent the next few days in a daze. She went through the motions at work, answered her friends' calls with half-hearted responses, and avoided any mention of Ryan altogether. She wasn't ready to talk about it yet. It was too raw, too painful. Her heart still ached, but more than that, her mind was in turmoil. She kept asking herself the same questions over and over: How had she missed the signs? How could she have been so blind?

In her apartment, Cat deleted every trace of Ryan. She erased his messages, deleted the pictures, and unfollowed him on social media. But no matter how much she tried to cleanse herself of him, there was one thing she couldn't delete: the lingering sense of betrayal. She had allowed herself to fall for him, to believe in the possibility of something real, only to discover that it had all been built on a foundation of lies.

Cat was torn between anger and sadness. She was angry at Ryan for betraying her trust, but she was also angry at herself for letting him. She felt stupid for ignoring all the red flags, for making excuses for his secrecy.

But the truth was, she had wanted to believe in him. She had wanted to believe that he was different, that their connection was real. Now, all that was left was the bitter taste of regret.

SCENE 2: UNRAVELLING the Past

After a week of emotional distance, Cat's curiosity got the better of her. Though she had ended things with Ryan, the questions still haunted her. Who was that woman? What was the "bigger thing" Ryan was involved in? And why had he been so evasive about his life? She realized she couldn't move on without answers, and as much as it hurt to dig deeper, she knew she needed closure.

Cat started by doing more research on Ryan. This time, she went beyond just social media and LinkedIn profiles. She began contacting mutual friends and acquaintances—people who might know more about him. The responses she received were mixed. Some people knew him as a charming, successful tech entrepreneur, while others seemed to have only a vague idea of who he was.

One afternoon, Cat received a message from an old college friend of Ryan's, a woman named Rebecca. Rebecca had seen Cat's post about their breakup and reached out with concern. They agreed to meet for coffee, and when they finally sat down together, Cat was struck by how much Rebecca seemed to know.

"I knew something wasn't right with Ryan," Rebecca said as she stirred her coffee. "We all did, honestly. He was always secretive, even in college. He never let anyone get too close."

Cat frowned. "But why? What was he hiding?"

Rebecca hesitated, glancing around as if she was about to share something she wasn't sure she should. "There were rumours," she said finally, her voice low. "Ryan wasn't always into tech. He used to hang out with some... shady people. Some of us thought he might be involved in something illegal, but no one ever had proof. He just always seemed to be operating in some grey area, you know?"

Cat's heart raced as she listened. This was the first real lead she had found—the first concrete suggestion that Ryan's secretive behaviour wasn't just about his work but something far more dangerous.

"Do you think he's still involved with those people?" Cat asked, her voice barely a whisper.

Rebecca shrugged. "I don't know. I haven't talked to him in years, but when I heard you were dating him, I couldn't help but worry. He has a way of pulling people into his world, making them believe he's something he's not."

Cat felt a chill run down her spine. She had fallen for Ryan's charm, just like everyone else. But now she was beginning to see that the man she had known was only a facade—one carefully constructed to hide whatever darkness lay beneath.

SCENE 3: CONFRONTING the Lies

Determined to confront Ryan one last time, Cat decided to meet with him face to face. She couldn't move on without fully understanding who he was and what had driven him to deceive her.

Cat sent Ryan a message, asking him to meet her at a park where they used to go when they first started dating. She wasn't sure if he would agree to it, but to her surprise, he responded almost immediately.

When Cat arrived at the park, Ryan was already there, sitting on a bench near the pond. His face was tense, his usual charm replaced by a solemn expression.

"I didn't expect to hear from you," Ryan said as Cat approached. "After everything... I figured you were done with me."

"I am," Cat replied, sitting down beside him. "But I need to know the truth, Ryan. No more lies. No more deflections. I want to know who you really are."

Ryan sighed, running a hand through his hair. "You know who I am, Cat. I've told you—"

"No," Cat interrupted, her voice firm. "I don't. You've told me bits and pieces, but they don't add up. I know you've been involved with people from your past—people who aren't exactly on the up-and-up. And I know that woman wasn't just some random person you were having dinner with. So stop pretending and just tell me the truth."

Ryan was silent for a long time, his gaze fixed on the pond in front of them. Cat could see the conflict in his eyes, the struggle between his desire to maintain control and the weight of the lies he had built. Finally, he spoke, his voice barely above a whisper.

"I'm not proud of who I used to be," Ryan admitted. "There were things I did—things I'm not proud of. I was young, reckless, and I got involved with people I shouldn't have. I thought I could walk away from it all when I started working in tech, but it's not that simple. The people I was involved with... they don't just let you leave."

Cat's heart pounded in her chest as she listened. This was more than she had ever expected. She had thought Ryan was just hiding another relationship, but now it seemed like he had been hiding an entire double life.

"So you're still involved with them?" Cat asked, her voice tight with fear.

Ryan nodded. "In a way. I don't want to be, but they still have leverage over me. That's why I've been so secretive, Cat. I didn't want to drag you into it. I thought I could protect you by keeping you out of that part of my life."

Cat shook her head, tears stinging her eyes. "You should have told me the truth from the beginning, Ryan. I would have understood. But instead, you lied to me. You made me feel like I was crazy for doubting you, when all along you were hiding this huge part of your life."

Ryan reached out to touch her hand, but Cat pulled away. "I'm sorry," he said softly. "I never meant to hurt you. I thought I could keep you safe by keeping you at a distance. But I see now that I was wrong."

Cat wiped away a tear, her emotions swirling inside her. She had wanted the truth, and now she had it. But the truth didn't make things any easier. It didn't erase the pain of Ryan's betrayal or the damage that had been done to their relationship.

"I can't be with someone who lies to me, Ryan," Cat said, her voice breaking. "I can't be with someone who's still involved in something dangerous. I deserve better than that."

Ryan nodded, his eyes filled with regret. "I understand. And I don't blame you for walking away. But I do care about you, Cat. I always have."

Cat stood up, her heart heavy. "Caring about someone isn't enough, Ryan. Not when it's built on lies."

With that, she turned and walked away, leaving Ryan sitting alone on the bench. As she walked through the park, Cat felt a sense of finality settle over her. She had gotten the answers she needed, but they hadn't brought her the closure she had hoped for. Instead, they had only confirmed what she had already known deep down: Ryan was never the man she thought he was.

SCENE 4: RECLAIMING Her Life

In the weeks that followed, Cat focused on reclaiming her life. She threw herself into her work, spent more time with her friends, and started picking up hobbies she had neglected during her relationship with Ryan. It wasn't easy—there were still moments when the pain of the betrayal would creep in, moments when she would miss the good times she had shared with Ryan. But those moments were becoming fewer and farther between.

Cat also started seeing a therapist, something she had never considered before. Talking through her feelings helped her process the emotional rollercoaster she had been on, and it gave her the tools to start healing. She began to realize that while Ryan's lies had hurt her deeply, they didn't define her. She was stronger than that, and she was capable of anything.

Chapter 7

The Turning Point

Scene 1: New Beginnings

The sound of waves crashing against the shore filled the air as Cat stood on the beach, her toes buried in the warm sand. She had come here to clear her head, to find some peace after the emotional upheaval of the last few months. The seaside had always been her sanctuary—a place where she could breathe, think, and reset.

It had been three months since her breakup with Ryan. In that time, Cat had worked hard to rebuild her life. She had moved to a new apartment in the city, one with big windows that let in natural light and a balcony that overlooked a small park. She had thrown herself into work with renewed energy, taking on new clients and projects that challenged her creatively. But most importantly, she had started reconnecting with herself, rediscovering the things that brought her joy.

The pain of Ryan's betrayal still lingered, but it no longer consumed her. Therapy had helped her process the experience, and she had come to understand that while Ryan had hurt her, she was not defined by his actions. She had also realized that she had fallen into the trap of losing herself in the relationship, putting Ryan's needs and secrets above her own well-being. It was a hard lesson to learn, but one she was grateful for in the end.

As she gazed out at the horizon, Cat felt a sense of calm wash over her. This was the turning point she had been waiting for—the moment when she could finally let go of the past and embrace the future. She wasn't the same person she had been before Ryan. She was stronger, wiser, and more in tune with what she wanted in life.

SCENE 2: UNEXPECTED Encounters

Later that day, as Cat was packing up her things to leave the beach, her phone buzzed in her bag. She pulled it out, expecting a message from a friend, but instead saw an unknown number on the screen. Frowning, she hesitated before answering.

"Hello?"

"Cat?" The voice on the other end was familiar, but it took her a moment to place it.

"Rebecca?" Cat asked, surprised.

"Yeah, it's me. I hope you don't mind me calling. I got your number from a mutual friend."

Cat wasn't sure how to feel about hearing from Rebecca, Ryan's old college friend who had given her the first real insight into his past. She had appreciated Rebecca's honesty back then, but she hadn't expected to hear from her again.

"What's up?" Cat asked, her curiosity piqued.

"I've been thinking a lot about our conversation a few months ago," Rebecca said, her tone serious. "And there's something I think you should know."

Cat's heart skipped a beat. She thought she had put everything behind her, but now Rebecca's words brought a rush of anxiety back to the surface. "What is it?"

"Ryan's been arrested," Rebecca said bluntly. "I'm not sure if you've heard, but it's all over the news. The people he was involved with... it all caught up to him."

Cat's mind reeled as she processed the information. Ryan, arrested? She hadn't heard anything about it, and she wasn't sure how to feel. On one hand, it confirmed what she had always suspected—that Ryan's secrets were tied to something much darker than she had initially realized. But on the other hand, it brought a sense of finality to the chapter she had been trying to close.

"What happened?" Cat asked, her voice tight with emotion.

"It turns out he was involved in some sort of money laundering scheme," Rebecca explained. "The authorities had been investigating him for a while, and they finally had enough evidence to bring him in. I'm sorry, Cat. I know this must be a lot to take in."

Cat nodded, though Rebecca couldn't see her. "Thank you for telling me. It's... it's a lot to process."

"If you ever want to talk, I'm here," Rebecca offered.

Cat appreciated the sentiment, but she wasn't sure she wanted to reopen the wounds that had taken so long to heal. "I'll keep that in mind," she said softly before ending the call.

As she sat on the sand, staring out at the ocean, Cat let the news sink in. Ryan's arrest was a shock, but it also brought with it a strange sense of closure. She had always known there was more to his story than he had let on, and now, the truth had come to light. It was messy, painful, and complicated, but at least it was no longer hidden in the shadows.

For the first time in a long time, Cat felt free. She had been living under the weight of Ryan's lies for so long that she hadn't realized how much it had affected her. Now, with the truth out in the open, she could finally move on without any lingering doubts or regrets.

SCENE 3: THE TURNING Point

In the weeks following Ryan's arrest, Cat found herself reflecting on the choices she had made over the past year. She had been through a lot—falling in love, being deceived, and then rebuilding herself piece by piece. But now, as she stood on the other side of it all, she realized something important: she was stronger than she had ever given herself credit for.

Cat had always been the kind of person who put others' needs before her own. She had been so eager to please, to make things work with Ryan, that she had ignored her own instincts and boundaries. But now, she knew better. She had learned the hard way that love wasn't supposed to be about sacrificing yourself for someone else's lies. Love was about honesty, respect, and mutual support—things she hadn't received from Ryan.

One evening, as Cat sat on her balcony, sipping a glass of wine and watching the sunset, she made a promise to herself. She promised that from now on, she would never settle for less than she deserved. She would trust her instincts, prioritize her own happiness, and never allow herself to be consumed by someone else's drama again.

It was a turning point for her—not just in her love life, but in every aspect of her life. She started setting clearer boundaries at work, speaking up for herself in ways she hadn't before. She began exploring new hobbies and passions, trying things she had always wanted to do but had never had the time or courage to pursue. She took a solo trip to a small coastal town, where she spent her days hiking, reading, and simply enjoying her own company.

And for the first time in a long time, Cat felt at peace.

SCENE 4: A NEW CONNECTION

As Cat continued to embrace her newfound independence, she began to open herself up to the idea of love again—but this time, on her own terms. She wasn't in a rush to find someone new, but she also wasn't closing herself off to the possibility. If the right person came along, she was ready to approach the relationship with the lessons she had learned.

One evening, while attending a friend's art exhibition, Cat found herself deep in conversation with a man named Alex. He was kind, intelligent, and easy to talk to, and there was a warmth about him that made Cat feel comfortable. Unlike Ryan, Alex didn't seem to be hiding anything. He was open and honest about his life, his career, and his passions.

They exchanged numbers at the end of the evening, and over the next few weeks, they began texting and meeting up for casual coffee dates. There was no rush, no pressure—just two people getting to know each other. Cat appreciated the slow pace. It gave her time to reflect on what she truly wanted in a relationship.

As she got to know Alex better, Cat realized that he embodied many of the qualities she had always admired but hadn't found in her past relationships. He was supportive, respectful, and attentive, and most importantly, he valued her independence. He didn't try to control or manipulate her—he simply enjoyed spending time with her, and that was enough.

For Cat, this was a turning point in how she viewed relationships. She had always believed that love had to be intense, passionate, and all-consuming, but now she saw things differently. Love didn't have to be about grand gestures or sweeping emotions. It could be about quiet moments of connection, mutual respect, and a sense of peace.

With Alex, there were no red flags, no secrets lurking in the background. There was only honesty and a shared desire to build something meaningful together.

Scene 5: Moving Forward

AS CAT AND ALEX'S RELATIONSHIP blossomed, Cat felt a sense of contentment that she hadn't experienced in a long time. It wasn't that her life was perfect—there were still challenges, setbacks, and difficult days—but she had learned how to navigate them with grace and resilience. She had learned how to trust herself again, and that made all the difference.

Looking back on her time with Ryan, Cat no longer felt the sting of betrayal. Instead, she felt gratitude for the lessons she had learned. She had grown in ways she never expected, and those experiences had shaped her into the person she was today—stronger, wiser, and more in tune with her own needs and desires.

Ryan's arrest had been the final chapter in a story that had once consumed her, but it was no longer the defining moment of her life. Cat had moved on, and she had found a new sense of purpose and joy. She had taken control of her own narrative, and she was excited to see where the next chapter would take her.

As she stood on her balcony one evening, watching the city lights twinkle in the distance, Cat smiled to herself. This was her turning point. And she was ready for whatever came next.

Chapter 8

Dangerously in Love

Scene 1: The New Normal

Cat's life had finally fallen into a rhythm she enjoyed. She was at peace with the past, and her relationship with Alex was blossoming into something steady and strong. It was a love that felt safe, nurturing, and honest—exactly what she needed after the tumultuous rollercoaster with Ryan.

Alex brought out the best in her. He supported her career ambitions, encouraged her creativity, and treated her with a kindness she had once thought was reserved only for fictional romances. Cat appreciated how effortlessly they clicked, how easy it was to be with him without the weight of secrets and lies. For once, there were no hidden agendas, no red flags waving in the background—just a simple, honest connection.

Despite this sense of comfort, however, there was still an itch Cat couldn't scratch—a lingering feeling she couldn't quite shake. The more stable things became with Alex, the more she found herself reflecting on the intensity of her past relationship with Ryan. As much as it had hurt her, she couldn't deny that the highs had been intoxicating. The passion, the drama, the undeniable spark—they had all made her feel alive in a way that her more tranquil love with Alex didn't. It was a dangerous thought, one that made her question herself.

Cat found herself staring at old photos late at night, revisiting moments with Ryan—wondering why, despite everything he had put her through, she couldn't fully erase him from her mind. Even though she knew their relationship had been built on deception, a part of her still craved the intensity that had defined their time together.

SCENE 2: A SUDDEN ENCOUNTER

One crisp autumn afternoon, Cat was walking down a crowded street in the city when she spotted something—or rather, someone—that made her heart stop. There, standing across the street, was Ryan.

Her breath caught in her throat. She hadn't seen him since their final conversation, when she had walked away from him at the park. She thought she'd never see him again, especially after hearing about his arrest. And yet, here he was, standing in the middle of her life again as if nothing had changed.

Cat froze, unsure of what to do. She could turn and walk away, pretend she hadn't seen him. But something in her wouldn't let her. Against her better judgment, she found herself stepping into the street and heading in his direction.

Ryan noticed her immediately. His eyes widened in surprise as their gazes locked, and for a moment, Cat thought she saw a flicker of guilt cross his face. But then, just as quickly, his familiar, charming smile returned.

"Cat," he said, his voice smooth and low as he closed the distance between them. "I didn't think I'd see you again."

"I didn't expect to see you either," Cat replied, her voice tight. She couldn't help but notice that despite everything, her body still reacted to him—the adrenaline rushing through her veins, her heart pounding in her chest.

"I was released on bail," Ryan explained, as if reading her thoughts. "I've been laying low, staying out of trouble."

"Trouble?" Cat scoffed. "Isn't that what your life is built on?"

Ryan sighed, rubbing the back of his neck. "Look, I know I hurt you. I lied to you, and I'll regret that for the rest of my life. But I never stopped caring about you, Cat. That was real."

Cat stared at him, anger and confusion swirling inside her. "It doesn't matter how much you cared, Ryan. What we had was based on lies."

"I know," he said softly, his eyes darkening with regret. "But I've changed, Cat. I've had a lot of time to think, and I realize now how much I messed up. I've cut ties with the people I was involved with. I'm trying to make things right."

Cat didn't know what to say. She didn't trust him—how could she? But there was something in his voice, something in the way he looked at her, that made her question everything she had told herself about him.

"Why are you telling me this?" she asked, her voice barely above a whisper.

"Because I never stopped loving you," Ryan admitted. "And I know it's too late, but I needed you to know."

Cat felt like the ground was shifting beneath her feet. She had convinced herself that she had moved on from Ryan, that her life with Alex was everything she wanted. But now, standing in front of Ryan again, hearing him say those words, she wasn't sure anymore.

She wanted to walk away, to leave him behind and return to the safe, stable life she had built. But a part of her—a part she had buried deep inside—still longed for the passion and intensity that had once defined their relationship.

"I can't do this," Cat said finally, shaking her head. "I've moved on, Ryan. I'm with someone else now."

Ryan's face fell, but he nodded in understanding. "I figured as much. I just... I had to try."

Cat turned to walk away, but as she did, Ryan called out to her one last time. "If you ever change your mind, Cat, you know where to find me."

Scene 3: Torn Between Two Worlds

After her encounter with Ryan, Cat found herself spiralling into a whirlwind of emotions. She had worked so hard to move on from him, to build a life with Alex that was healthy and fulfilling. But now, the cracks were beginning to show. The love she had with Alex was safe, but it lacked the fire she had once felt with Ryan.

For days, Cat was consumed by thoughts of Ryan. She knew it was dangerous to entertain them, but she couldn't help it. The passion they had shared was unlike anything she had ever experienced before, and part of her wondered if she would ever feel that way again.

At the same time, she couldn't deny how good Alex was for her. He was steady, reliable, and honest. He treated her with the respect and kindness she had always wanted in a partner. And yet, she found herself questioning whether it was enough.

Cat's internal conflict began to spill over into her relationship with Alex. She became distant, distracted, and unable to fully engage in their conversations or plans for the future. Alex noticed the change in her, and though he tried to be understanding, it was clear that he was hurt.

One evening, after a particularly tense dinner, Alex confronted her. "Cat, what's going on? You've been distant lately. Is something wrong?"

Cat hesitated, unsure of how to explain the turmoil inside her. She didn't want to hurt Alex—he didn't deserve that. But she also couldn't ignore the fact that her feelings for Ryan were resurfacing in ways she hadn't expected.

"I don't know," Cat admitted, her voice trembling. "I just... I've been feeling conflicted. I thought I had moved on from my past, but seeing Ryan again... it's bringing up a lot of old feelings."

Alex's expression softened as he reached across the table to take her hand. "I get it, Cat. I know what you went through with Ryan was intense. But I need to know—do you still have feelings for him?"

Cat looked down at their intertwined hands, her heart aching with guilt. "I don't know," she whispered. "I thought I was over him, but now... I'm not so sure."

Alex's grip on her hand tightened, but his voice remained calm. "I love you, Cat. And I want to be with you. But if you're not sure, if you're still torn between me and Ryan, then we need to figure this out. I don't want to be in a relationship where your heart isn't fully in it."

Tears welled up in Cat's eyes as she nodded. She knew Alex was right. She couldn't keep living in limbo, torn between two very different worlds. She had to make a decision, even if it meant risking everything.

SCENE 4: THE BREAKING Point

Cat spent the next few days in a state of emotional turmoil. She knew she couldn't keep stringing Alex along while her feelings for Ryan lingered in the background. She had to confront her emotions head-on, no matter how painful it might be.

One evening, after much soul-searching, Cat made the difficult decision to end things with Alex. She loved him—there was no doubt about that—but she couldn't ignore the part of herself that still yearned for the passion and excitement she had once shared with Ryan.

As they sat down to talk, Cat could see the hurt in Alex's eyes before she even said a word. He had been bracing himself for this conversation, and though it broke her heart to hurt him, she knew it was the right thing to do.

"I care about you so much, Alex," Cat began, her voice shaky with emotion. "But I've realized that I'm not being fair to you—or to myself. I'm still holding on to feelings from my past, and I can't fully commit to our relationship while those feelings are unresolved."

Alex's face was a mixture of pain and understanding. He nodded slowly, his eyes filled with sadness. "I appreciate your honesty, Cat. I just wish things could have been different."

"So do I," Cat whispered, tears streaming down her cheeks. "You deserve someone who can give you their whole heart, and right now, I'm not in a place to do that."

They sat in silence for a few moments, both grieving the loss of a relationship that had been good in so many ways but ultimately wasn't meant to last.

SCENE 5: DANGEROUSLY in Love

With Alex out of her life, Cat found herself drawn back into Ryan's orbit. It was dangerous, she knew that. But the intensity of their connection was something she couldn't resist. Ryan had always been like a drug to her—one she knew was bad for her, but one she couldn't seem to quit.

They began seeing each other again, slowly at first, testing the waters to see if anything had truly changed. Ryan was more open now, more willing to be honest about his past mistakes. He told her about the therapy he had been going through, the steps he was taking to distance himself from his old life.

For a while, it seemed like things might actually work out between them. The passion was still there, burning as brightly as ever, but this time it was tempered by a newfound sense of vulnerability. They were both older, wiser, and more aware of the dangers that had torn them apart before.

But as the weeks went on, Cat began to realize that some things never truly changed. Ryan was still reckless, still drawn to the thrill of danger. He still had secrets, and though he tried to keep them from Cat, she could sense that they were there, lurking just beneath the surface.

The more she tried to convince herself that things were different now, the more she realized that she was falling into the same patterns as before. She was dangerously in love with a man who couldn't fully be trusted—a man who had the power to pull her back into the darkness she had fought so hard to escape.

SCENE 6: THE FINAL Decision

As Cat stood on the edge of the abyss, she knew she had to make a choice—one that would determine the course of her life. She could stay with Ryan, continue to be swept up in the whirlwind of passion and danger that defined their relationship, or she could walk away for good, finally breaking free from the cycle of love and lies.

It was the hardest decision she had ever faced. But deep down, Cat knew that if she stayed with Ryan, she would only end up hurting herself again. She had learned too much, grown too much, to let herself fall back into the same trap.

One night, as they sat together in Ryan's apartment, Cat took a deep breath and looked into his eyes. "I love you, Ryan," she said softly. "I always will. But I can't keep doing this."

Ryan's face fell, and for a moment, he looked like the lost boy she had once fallen in love with. "Cat, please..."

But Cat shook her head. "I can't keep living in a world of secrets and danger. I need stability, honesty, and trust. And I don't think we can ever have that."

Ryan looked away, his jaw clenched with frustration. He knew she was right. He had always known it. But that didn't make it any easier to let her go.

"I'm sorry," Cat whispered, tears welling up in her eyes. "I can't do this anymore."

With that, she stood up and walked out of Ryan's apartment, her heart breaking with every step. It was the hardest thing she had ever done, but she knew it was the only way to save herself.

As Cat stepped out into the cool night air, she felt a strange sense of relief wash over her. For the first time in a long time, she was free—free from the toxic love that had held her captive for so long.

It wasn't going to be easy, and there would be days when she missed the thrill of being dangerously in love. But in the end, Cat knew that she had made the right choice.

She had chosen herself.

Chapter 9

The Big Betrayal

Scene 1: **A Fresh Start**

Cat was determined to start anew after walking away from Ryan. She was focusing on herself, her career, and regaining the stability she had been missing for so long. Her friends noticed the change in her, and for the first time in a long time, Cat felt proud of her decisions. She had broken free from the toxic cycle that had held her captive, and she was ready to rebuild her life.

Still, a part of her remained haunted by the ghost of her relationship with Ryan. She tried not to dwell on it, but certain moments brought back flashes of their time together. The tension in their relationship had been addictive, and while she knew it wasn't healthy, there were days when she missed the thrill.

One afternoon, while sipping coffee at her favourite café, Cat received a message on her phone. It was from Ryan. He hadn't reached out since their breakup, and seeing his name pop up on her screen sent her heart racing.

Can we talk? the message read.

Cat hesitated, her fingers hovering over the keyboard. She had done so well moving on from him, but now, here he was, pulling her back into his orbit. She couldn't help but wonder what he wanted. Was he trying to lure her back in? Or was there something more to it?

After a long pause, Cat typed a short reply: "What do you want, Ryan?"

The response came almost immediately. "It's not what you think. I just need to talk to you. It's important."

Cat felt a knot form in her stomach. Part of her wanted to ignore him, to pretend that he didn't exist. But her curiosity got the better of her. She agreed to meet him later that evening, against her better judgment.

SCENE 2: THE REVELATION

They met at a quiet bar on the outskirts of town. The atmosphere was low-key, with dim lighting and soft jazz playing in the background. Cat walked in, her heart pounding in her chest, and spotted Ryan sitting in a booth at the back of the room. He looked different—more worn, like he had been through hell since the last time they had seen each other.

As soon as Cat sat down, Ryan cut to the chase. "I know you don't trust me, Cat. And you have every right not to. But I need to tell you something—something I should have told you a long time ago."

Cat crossed her arms defensively. "Go on."

Ryan took a deep breath, his hands shaking slightly as he reached into his jacket pocket. He pulled out a small, weathered envelope and slid it across the table toward her.

"What's this?" Cat asked, eyeing the envelope suspiciously.

"It's the truth," Ryan said, his voice strained. "I've been keeping something from you—something that goes beyond our relationship. I didn't know how to tell you before, but you deserve to know."

Cat hesitated before opening the envelope. Inside, she found a stack of documents—legal papers, bank statements, and other official-looking forms. As she flipped through them, her eyes widened in disbelief.

"What the hell is this?" Cat whispered, her voice trembling.

"It's about your father," Ryan said quietly. "He wasn't just some random businessman. He was involved in things—dangerous things.

And when I first met you, I was working for people who were looking into his dealings. They sent me to get close to you."

Cat felt like the floor had been pulled out from under her. She had always believed that her relationship with Ryan, despite its flaws, had been based on genuine feelings. But now, it seemed like it had all been a lie—a carefully constructed plan to manipulate her.

"You were using me?" Cat's voice cracked with disbelief. "From the very beginning?"

Ryan shook his head desperately. "At first, yes. I won't lie to you—I was sent to find out what you knew about your father's business dealings. But things changed, Cat. I fell in love with you. That was real."

Cat stared at him, her mind racing. "But you kept this from me. You let me believe that everything between us was real when it was all a setup?"

Ryan reached across the table, trying to take her hand, but Cat recoiled. "I didn't know how to tell you," he said, his voice full of regret. "But I swear to you, I stopped working for those people a long time ago. I tried to protect you."

"Protect me?" Cat scoffed. "You betrayed me, Ryan. You've been lying to me this whole time."

Tears welled up in Cat's eyes as the weight of the betrayal settled in. Everything she had known, everything she had felt for Ryan, was now tainted by this revelation. He hadn't just hurt her—he had used her, manipulated her, and now, she was left to pick up the pieces.

SCENE 3: THE FALLOUT

Cat left the bar in a daze, her mind reeling from the truth Ryan had revealed. She didn't know where to go or who to turn to. The revelation about her father was shocking enough, but the fact that Ryan had been involved from the very beginning—that he had been sent to manipulate her—was a betrayal she couldn't forgive.

For the next few days, Cat shut herself off from the world. She couldn't focus on work, she avoided her friends, and she barely left her apartment. All she could think about was how stupid she had been to trust Ryan. Even after everything they had been through, she had allowed herself to believe that there was still some good in him. Now, she realized how naive she had been.

But as the shock began to wear off, Cat found herself consumed by a different emotion: anger. Ryan had lied to her, manipulated her, and betrayed her in the worst possible way. But she wasn't going to let him get away with it. She had been played, but she wasn't going to be a victim anymore.

Cat began digging into her father's past, determined to uncover the truth about his business dealings and the people who had targeted her. She poured over the documents Ryan had given her, trying to piece together the puzzle. The more she uncovered, the more she realized that her father had been involved in something far bigger—and far more dangerous—than she had ever imagined.

SCENE 4: CONFRONTATION

With her newfound knowledge, Cat decided it was time to confront Ryan one last time. She needed answers—real answers this time—and she wasn't going to let him off the hook without a fight. She arranged to meet him at his apartment, determined to get to the bottom of everything. When she arrived, Ryan seemed nervous, as if he knew what was coming. He opened the door for her, but Cat could see the tension in his shoulders, the way he avoided her gaze.

"Why did you do it, Ryan?" Cat demanded as soon as she stepped inside. "Why did you lie to me? Why did you use me?"

Ryan sighed heavily and ran a hand through his hair. "I didn't want to hurt you, Cat. I swear I didn't. But I was in too deep. I couldn't just walk away from the people I was working for. They were dangerous."

"So you just decided to manipulate me instead?" Cat shot back, her voice filled with anger. "You could have told me the truth. You could have trusted me."

"I couldn't," Ryan said, his voice pleading. "You don't understand, Cat. These people—they don't just walk away. I was trying to protect you."

"By lying to me? By using me?" Cat shook her head in disbelief. "You weren't protecting me, Ryan. You were protecting yourself."

Ryan looked down at the floor, his face filled with guilt. "I know I messed up, Cat. But I did love you. That part was real."

Cat's heart ached at his words, but she couldn't bring herself to believe him anymore. The trust between them was shattered beyond repair.

"Love isn't supposed to feel like this," Cat said softly, her voice trembling. "Love isn't supposed to hurt this much."

Ryan looked up at her, his eyes filled with regret. "I'm sorry, Cat. I'm so sorry."

But it was too late. The damage had been done, and there was no going back. Cat knew that she couldn't keep letting Ryan back into her life—not after everything he had done. She had to move on, once and for all.

Without another word, Cat turned and walked out of Ryan's apartment, leaving him behind for good. As she stepped into the cool night air, she felt a sense of finality wash over her. The chapter with Ryan was finally closed, and now, it was time for her to move forward—on her own terms.

SCENE 5: A NEW BEGINNING

In the weeks that followed, Cat slowly began to rebuild her life. She threw herself into her work, reconnecting with her friends and focusing on her own happiness. The betrayal had left scars, but Cat was determined not to let it define her.

She had learned a lot about herself throughout the ordeal—about her strength, her resilience, and her ability to move on from even the deepest of betrayals. She wasn't the same person she had been when she first met Ryan. She was stronger now, more self-assured, and more aware of her own worth.

And as she stood on the edge of this new chapter in her life, Cat knew that she would be okay. She had been through hell and back, but she had come out the other side stronger than ever.

This was her story now—a story

of survival, of growth, and of finding her own way in the world.

The end was just the beginning.

Chapter 10

The Comeback

Scene 1: Picking Up the Pieces

The weeks following Ryan's betrayal had been some of the hardest of Cat's life. She had to confront a painful truth: the man she thought she loved had been lying to her from the very beginning, using her as a pawn in a dangerous game she didn't even know she was playing. But as difficult as it was, Cat had learned to move forward.

She focused on healing. She returned to her routines, spent time with her friends, and began pouring her energy into her work. She was building her confidence back, reclaiming her independence. But even though she was making progress, there was still a piece of her that was restless—something unresolved, something waiting to be confronted.

Cat knew that this chapter of her life couldn't close until she had taken control of the narrative. She couldn't just let things happen to her; she needed to make a comeback.

She was ready for the next chapter—a chapter she would write herself.

SCENE 2: THE RETURN of the Past

One evening, Cat received an unexpected call from a private investigator she had hired to look deeper into her father's affairs. After Ryan's confession, Cat had been determined to uncover the full truth about her father's business dealings, and she had wanted answers.

The investigator's voice was serious as he delivered the news: "Cat, there's something you need to know. Your father's business dealings weren't just dangerous—they were tied to some very powerful people. People who may not want the truth coming out."

Cat felt a chill run down her spine. "What does that mean for me?"

"It means you need to be careful," the investigator said. "These people aren't afraid to go after anyone who might expose them. And now that you're digging into your father's past, you're on their radar."

Cat's mind raced. She had suspected that her father's business had been shady, but she had no idea how deep it ran. Now, it seemed that she had gotten herself involved in something far more dangerous than she had anticipated.

But Cat wasn't one to back down. She had spent too much of her life being manipulated by others—by Ryan, by the secrets of her father's past. This time, she wasn't going to let anyone control her fate.

SCENE 3: RISING FROM the Ashes

Determined not to be intimidated, Cat began to dig deeper into her father's connections. She met with the investigator again and started piecing together the puzzle that had haunted her family for years.

It wasn't long before she uncovered the full extent of the truth: her father had been involved with an international crime syndicate, using his business as a front for money laundering, illegal arms deals, and more. He had tried to shield her from it, but his actions had left a trail, and now Cat had found herself in the crosshairs of powerful enemies.

But Cat wasn't going to let fear stop her. She knew she had to take action—both to protect herself and to finally put an end to the dangerous legacy her father had left behind.

She began working with law enforcement, providing them with the information she had uncovered. It wasn't easy—every step she took felt like a dangerous gamble—but Cat was determined to see it through.

Her comeback wasn't just about getting back at Ryan or moving on from the past—it was about taking control of her life in a way she never had before.

SCENE 4: THE FINAL Confrontation

As Cat's investigation continued, she found herself being followed. There were strange cars parked outside her apartment, shadowy figures watching her from a distance. She was being threatened—warnings meant to scare her off.

But Cat didn't back down. She was too close to the truth now to stop.

One night, after a particularly unnerving encounter with a man who had been following her, Cat decided to confront the people behind it all. She had uncovered the name of one of the syndicate's key players—a man named Victor Kozlov—and she knew she had to meet with him directly if she wanted to end this once and for all.

Cat arranged a meeting through one of her father's old contacts. It was dangerous, but she was prepared. She had taken precautions—alerted the authorities, set up backup plans—and now it was time to face the people who had been haunting her.

The meeting took place in an abandoned warehouse on the outskirts of the city. The tension was thick as Cat stepped inside, her heart pounding in her chest. She was greeted by Victor, a tall man with cold, calculating eyes.

"You've been making trouble for us," Victor said, his voice low and menacing. "I suggest you stop before things get worse for you."

Cat squared her shoulders and met his gaze. "I'm not afraid of you. I'm not going to stop until the truth comes out."

Victor studied her for a moment before smirking. "You're brave, I'll give you that. But bravery only gets you so far. You don't know what you're up against."

"I know enough," Cat replied, her voice steady. "And I'm not backing down."

Victor's smirk faded, replaced by a steely expression. "Then you leave me no choice."

Just as he spoke, the warehouse doors burst open, and law enforcement agents swarmed in. Cat had set the trap perfectly—Victor and his associates were arrested on the spot, caught red-handed in the middle of their criminal dealings.

As the authorities took Victor away, Cat felt a sense of relief wash over her. She had faced the danger head-on and come out on top. The chapter of her father's dark legacy was finally coming to a close, and Cat had been the one to bring it down.

SCENE 5: THE COMEBACK

With Victor and his syndicate behind bars, Cat's life slowly began to return to normal. The investigation had taken a toll on her, but she was stronger for it. She had faced betrayal, danger, and uncertainty, but she had emerged from it all with a newfound sense of purpose.

Cat's story wasn't just one of survival—it was one of triumph. She had taken control of her life in ways she never imagined possible, and now she was ready for whatever came next.

She reconnected with her friends, rebuilt her career, and even started dating again—this time, with a newfound sense of clarity and self-worth. She knew what she wanted in life, and she wasn't willing to settle for anything less.

And as she stood at the edge of this new chapter, Cat couldn't help but feel a sense of pride. She had made her comeback—not just from the betrayal of a toxic relationship, but from the shadows of her father's past. She had reclaimed her story, and now it was hers to write.

SCENE 6: THE FUTURE

Months passed, and Cat continued to rebuild her life. The investigation into her father's dealings had made headlines, and Cat had become something of a local hero for her role in bringing down the syndicate. She had even started a blog, sharing her story and encouraging others to take control of their own lives.

Her comeback had resonated with people, and Cat found herself receiving messages from women who had gone through similar experiences—women who had faced betrayal, danger, and uncertainty, but who had found the strength to rise above it all.

Cat's story wasn't over yet. She knew there would be new challenges, new obstacles to overcome. But she also knew that she was ready for them. She had faced the worst, and she had come out stronger on the other side.

And as she looked toward the future, Cat knew one thing for certain: she was in control of her own destiny now. Whatever came next, she would face it with strength, courage, and an unshakable belief in herself.

Her comeback was only the beginning.

Chapter 11

The Reconciliation

Scene 1: The Unexpected Call

It had been nearly a year since Cat brought down the syndicate and put the darkest parts of her past behind her. Life had returned to something resembling normalcy. She was thriving in her career, building her personal brand as a speaker and writer. Her story had become an inspiration to many, but beneath her success, there was still a lingering sense of unfinished business.

One afternoon, while sitting at her desk, Cat received an unexpected phone call. The name on the caller ID sent a jolt through her—*Ryan*. It had been months since she last heard from him. The sound of his voice immediately brought back a flood of memories, both good and bad.

"H-hello, Cat?" Ryan's voice was hesitant, almost vulnerable. "It's me. I know I'm the last person you want to hear from, but I need to talk to you."

Cat's heart raced. She thought she had closed that chapter of her life, but hearing Ryan's voice stirred something deep inside her—something unresolved.

"I'm not sure what there is to say," Cat replied cautiously. "We said everything the last time we spoke."

"I know," Ryan admitted. "I've had a lot of time to think since then. I messed up, Cat. I've been in therapy, trying to sort through everything. I know I don't deserve a second chance, but... could we meet? Just to talk. No pressure."

Cat hesitated. Part of her wanted to shut him out, to protect herself from any more pain. But another part of her was curious. She had always believed in second chances—for others and for herself. Maybe this was her opportunity to find closure.

"Alright," Cat finally said. "But just to talk."

They arranged to meet the following weekend at a small café near the waterfront, a place that held no memories for them, neutral territory. As soon as she hung up, Cat felt a swirl of emotions—nervousness, anger, but also a faint hope. Could this be the reconciliation she needed, or was she inviting more heartache?

SCENE 2: FACING THE Past

The day of the meeting arrived, and Cat approached the café with a mix of apprehension and curiosity. Ryan was already seated when she arrived, looking different—older, a little worn, but there was a softness in his eyes that hadn't been there before.

"Cat," he said quietly as she sat down. "Thank you for meeting me."

Cat nodded, her expression guarded. "You said you wanted to talk. So talk."

Ryan took a deep breath. "I've spent a lot of time thinking about what I did—how I hurt you. It's haunted me every day since you walked out of my life. And I want you to know that I'm truly, deeply sorry. Not just for the lies, but for everything. I was selfish. I let my fear and greed control me, and I betrayed the only person I've ever truly loved."

Cat felt a pang in her chest at his words, but she didn't let it show. She had heard apologies before—empty ones that meant nothing. This time, she needed more than words.

"I appreciate your apology, Ryan," Cat said evenly. "But the truth is, you didn't just hurt me. You broke my trust in a way that can't be easily repaired. You used me, manipulated me, and lied to me about everything. I've had to rebuild myself from the ground up because of you."

Ryan nodded, his eyes filled with regret. "I know. And I don't expect you to forgive me. I just wanted you to know that I've changed. I'm not the man I used to be."

Cat studied him for a moment, searching for any signs of insincerity. She could see that he was different—more humbled, more self-aware. But she wasn't ready to let him back into her life so easily.

"I'm glad you've changed," Cat said finally. "But that doesn't mean we can go back to the way things were."

"I don't expect that," Ryan said quickly. "I just wanted a chance to make things right—to apologize in person and maybe, if you're willing, to start over as friends. No lies, no manipulation. Just honesty."

Cat considered his offer. Could she truly let him back into her life, even as a friend? It was a risk, but perhaps it was a risk worth taking—for closure, for healing, for her own peace of mind.

"Alright," Cat said after a long pause. "We can try. But on my terms. And if I see any signs of the old you, I'm done. No second chances."

Ryan smiled, a look of relief washing over his face. "Thank you, Cat. I promise, I won't let you down this time."

Scene 3: Rebuilding Trust

The next few weeks were strange for Cat. She and Ryan began meeting for coffee occasionally, keeping things light and friendly. She was cautious, wary of letting him too close again, but she also found herself surprised by how different he seemed.

Ryan was open and honest about his past, his therapy sessions, and the work he was doing to better himself. He never pushed Cat to rekindle their romance, instead focusing on rebuilding trust one step at a time. Slowly, Cat began to let her guard down, allowing herself to see Ryan not as the man who had betrayed her, but as someone who was genuinely trying to make amends.

One evening, after they had spent the day walking through the city and talking about everything from work to life's small joys, Ryan looked at Cat with a serious expression. "I know I don't deserve to ask this, but do you ever think about us? About what could have been?"

Cat felt her heart skip a beat. She had been thinking about it more than she wanted to admit, but the scars of the past still held her back.

"I do think about it," Cat admitted. "But I also think about everything that happened. It's hard to imagine going back to that place."

Ryan nodded, understanding in his eyes. "I get it. And I won't push you. I just want you to know that, no matter what happens, I'm grateful for this second chance—whatever form it takes."

Cat smiled softly, appreciating his honesty. She wasn't ready for a relationship with Ryan again—not yet. But she could see that he had changed, and for the first time, she began to entertain the possibility that maybe, just maybe, they could find their way back to each other one day.

SCENE 4: THE RECKONING

As Cat and Ryan continued to rebuild their friendship, an unexpected threat from the past re-emerged. One evening, Cat received a chilling email—an anonymous message warning her to stop digging into her father's past or face the consequences.

Panic surged through her. She had thought the danger was behind her, that with Victor and his associates in prison, she was safe. But now, it seemed that there were still people out there who wanted to keep the truth buried.

Without hesitation, Cat reached out to Ryan. He had connections, resources, and experience with the darker side of life that she didn't. When she told him about the email, his face darkened.

"You're not dealing with amateurs," Ryan said grimly. "They're still watching, still waiting for an opportunity. We need to be careful."

For the first time since their reconciliation, Cat found herself leaning on Ryan again—not as a romantic partner, but as an ally. Together, they began to strategize, working with law enforcement and tightening their security. Cat knew she couldn't let fear control her life, but the threat was real, and she needed to protect herself.

Ryan was by her side every step of the way, his determination to keep her safe unwavering. It was during this time that Cat began to see the full scope of his transformation. He was no longer the selfish, manipulative man she had known. He was someone who truly cared about her, someone who was willing to put his own life on the line to protect her.

As they faced this new danger together, the walls between them began to crumble. Cat found herself drawn to Ryan in ways she hadn't expected. There was still chemistry between them, still an undeniable connection. But this time, it felt different—healthier, more honest.

Scene 5: The Choice

After weeks of uncertainty, the threat finally subsided. The authorities had identified the source of the emails and arrested those responsible. Once again, Cat's life returned to normal, but this time, things felt different.

She and Ryan had grown closer during the ordeal, and Cat found herself at a crossroads. She had seen the man Ryan had become—the man who had worked tirelessly to earn her trust back, the man who had stood by her side when things got dangerous. And she couldn't deny that her feelings for him had deepened.

One evening, as they sat on a bench overlooking the city, Ryan turned to Cat with a serious expression. "I know I said I wouldn't push, but I have to ask... do you think there's a chance for us? I'm not asking for an answer now, but I need to know if you feel what I feel."

Cat looked into his eyes, her heart racing. She had been wrestling with this question for weeks, and now, she was finally ready to face it.

"I don't know what the future holds," Cat said softly. "But I do know that I care about you, Ryan. You've changed. I've seen it. And I think... maybe we could try again."

Ryan's face lit up with hope, but he didn't rush to embrace her. Instead, he reached out and

gently took her hand. "We'll take it slow," he promised. "No pressure. Just us, figuring it out together."

Cat smiled, feeling a sense of peace wash over her. She wasn't sure where this path would lead, but for the first time in a long time, she felt ready to take the leap.

SCENE 6: A NEW BEGINNING

In the months that followed, Cat and Ryan began to rebuild their relationship, this time on a foundation of honesty, trust, and mutual respect. It wasn't always easy—there were moments of doubt, moments when the past threatened to resurface—but they faced each challenge together, hand in hand.

Their love story wasn't perfect, but it was real. It was a story of second chances, of growth, of healing. And as they moved forward, Cat knew that whatever the future held, they would face it together.

The reconciliation wasn't just about them finding their way back to each other—it was about finding themselves. Both Cat and Ryan had learned valuable lessons about love, trust, and forgiveness, and now, they were ready to write the next chapter of their lives.

Together.

Chapter 12
Epilogue

Scene 1: One Year Later

The soft hum of conversation filled the air at a cozy café on a quiet street corner, where the late afternoon sun cast a warm glow through the windows. Cat Sinclair sat at a small table by the window, gazing out at the world passing by. She had come a long way since the tumultuous events of the past few years—more than she ever could have imagined.

Her life had finally reached a point of balance and peace. The drama of her entanglement with Ryan, the betrayals, and the dangers they faced now felt like a distant memory, even though it had only been a year since the threats had subsided. She had re-established her career, launching a podcast where she spoke about resilience, healing, and personal transformation—sharing her story with thousands of listeners who found strength in her journey.

The café door opened with a soft chime, and Ryan walked in. He looked different—more relaxed, more at ease in his own skin. He smiled when he saw Cat, and she smiled back. Though they had rebuilt their relationship carefully, with patience and respect, the connection between them had grown deeper and stronger. It wasn't just about love anymore—it was about partnership, trust, and genuine companionship.

"Hey," Ryan said as he approached the table and took a seat across from her. "Sorry I'm late. Traffic was crazy."

Cat shook her head, her smile widening. "You're not late. I was just enjoying the view."

Ryan chuckled softly, then took her hand across the table. "I've been thinking a lot lately," he said, his voice thoughtful. "About how far we've come."

Cat nodded, her fingers gently squeezing his. "It's been quite a journey, hasn't it?"

"I never thought I'd get a second chance," Ryan admitted. "With you, with myself. I'm still working on things, but I'm grateful every day that we've made it to this point."

Cat smiled warmly, her eyes locking with his. "We both put in the work. And look where we are now."

SCENE 2: REFLECTIONS on Growth

As they sat together in the café, the conversation turned to reflections on the past year—their highs and lows, the moments of doubt, and the victories they had shared. Ryan had continued his therapy, and though the road wasn't always easy, he had managed to build a life he could be proud of. He had started a new job with a clean slate and had even become an advocate for mental health and personal growth, volunteering at local organizations to help others who had gone through similar struggles.

Cat, on the other hand, had found a sense of fulfillment she hadn't anticipated. Her podcast had taken off in ways she couldn't have imagined, allowing her to connect with people from all walks of life who found inspiration in her story. She had even started writing a book, detailing her journey from heartbreak to healing. It wasn't just about Ryan, but about everything she had learned—about herself, about love, and about the power of forgiveness.

"What's the title of your book again?" Ryan asked, grinning. "I want to make sure I get it right when I tell people I know the author."

Cat laughed, rolling her eyes playfully. "It's called *The Heart's Journey*. And no, it's not all about you," she teased.

Ryan chuckled, leaning back in his chair. "Good to know. But seriously, Cat, I'm proud of you. You've done something incredible."

Cat blushed slightly, still not entirely used to accepting praise. "Thank you. It's been a lot of work, but it's been worth it."

Their conversation meandered, touching on the little things—how they spent their weekends, the new hobbies they had picked up, and their plans for the future. For the first time in a long time, the future didn't feel like a source of anxiety. It felt like a wide-open space, full of possibilities.

SCENE 3: A FRESH START

After their coffee, Cat and Ryan took a walk along the waterfront. The sun was beginning to set, casting the sky in shades of pink and orange. They strolled hand-in-hand, the breeze cool against their skin as they watched the gentle waves lap against the shore.

"Do you ever think about what's next for us?" Ryan asked, breaking the comfortable silence.

Cat glanced at him, a soft smile on her lips. "Sometimes," she admitted. "But I've learned not to overthink it. We're in a good place now, and I'm happy. Whatever comes next, we'll figure it out together."

Ryan nodded, seeming content with that answer. "You're right. I just want you to know that I'm committed to this—to us."

Cat stopped walking and turned to face him, her expression serious but tender. "I know, Ryan. And I'm committed too. But I also think we've learned that we don't have to rush anything. We can take our time and let things unfold naturally."

Ryan smiled, pulling her into a gentle embrace. "I love you, Cat."

Cat's heart swelled with warmth, and she wrapped her arms around him. "I love you too, Ryan."

SCENE 4: EMBRACING the Future

As the sun dipped below the horizon, Cat and Ryan stood by the water, watching the last light of day fade into twilight. The air was calm, and the world around them seemed to hold its breath for a moment of stillness.

Cat thought about everything that had brought her to this point—the heartbreak, the betrayal, the fear, and the uncertainty. But she also thought about the strength she had found within herself, the courage it took to rebuild her life, and the love she had rediscovered in the most unexpected of ways.

Her journey wasn't over—not by a long shot. But she was ready for whatever came next, confident in herself and in the relationship she had worked so hard to rebuild.

As she stood there with Ryan, looking out at the vast expanse of water before them, Cat realized that this wasn't the end of her story. It was just the beginning of a new chapter—one filled with hope, love, and endless possibilities.

And for the first time in a long time, she felt at peace with where she was and excited for what the future held.

Final Scene: Moving Forward

In the days that followed, life continued to move forward. Cat's book was published to great acclaim, resonating with readers who saw themselves in her journey of love and resilience. Her podcast grew even more popular, becoming a platform for people to share their own stories of overcoming adversity.

Ryan continued to thrive in his personal and professional life, making amends for his past mistakes and building a future he could be proud of. Together, he and Cat supported each other in their individual growth, never losing sight of the lessons they had learned along the way.

Their relationship wasn't perfect, but it was real. It was built on trust, communication, and a deep understanding of one another. And as they looked ahead to the future, they knew that whatever challenges or surprises life threw their way, they would face them together—stronger, wiser, and more in love than ever before.

END...

Don't miss out!

Visit the website below and you can sign up to receive emails whenever Nazreen zainab publishes a new book. There's no charge and no obligation.

https://books2read.com/r/B-A-NKTJC-KTHYE

BOOKS2READ

Connecting independent readers to independent writers.